# TITLE II-A

This

BOOK

is

DEDICATED

To

Christopher

Knight

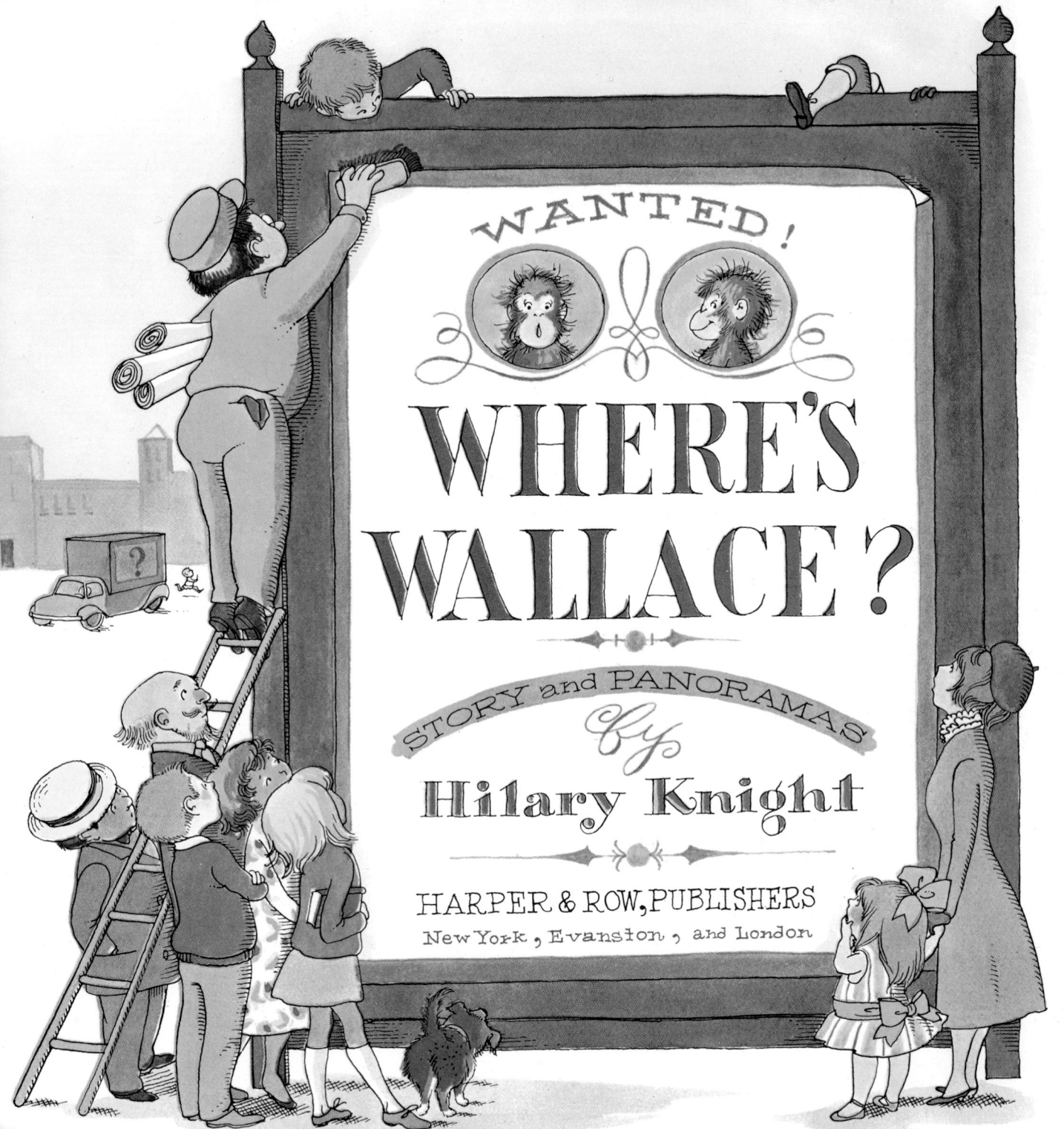

WANTED!

# WHERE'S WALLACE?

STORY and PANORAMAS

*of*

## Hilary Knight

HARPER & ROW, PUBLISHERS
New York, Evanston, and London

Standard Book Number 06-023170-X (Trade Edition)
Standard Book Number 06-023171-8 (Harpercrest Edition)

**W**allace was an ape. To be exact, an orangutan. He had beautiful long orange fur and bright black eyes.

Wallace lived in a little zoo in a big busy city. He was so happy and friendly that his cage was always surrounded with laughing people.

If you wanted to find Wallace at the zoo, it wouldn't be difficult. You would simply follow all the people

like this . . . . . . . .

Everyone loved Wallace and Wallace loved everyone. He was especially fond of his keeper, Mr. Frumbee, a plump little man who treated Wallace as if he were one of his own family.

He provided all the things Wallace needed as well as a weekly allowance which Wallace kept in a bank.

They were fast dear friends who often enjoyed

having a bite to eat together

or reading

or simply having a good time.

Yet Wallace longed to get out of his cage and see the world around him. He wanted to do all the things other people do. He would have liked to have fine clothes—the kind the gentlemen wore who came to see him.

One afternoon when most of the visitors had left the zoo, Wallace's keeper, Mr. Frumbee, went to feed the elephants.

Wallace sat and gazed at his cage door. Look! It was open a crack.

"No one will miss me for a few hours," he thought. Taking his bank, he scrambled out of his cage and over to an elegantly dressed man.

"Where can I find a splendid suit like the one you have on, sir?" he asked.

"Bumpus Brothers' Department Store," answered the surprised man, and with that Wallace was off.

"Come back, come back," the man cried, drawing quite a crowd—including Wallace's keeper.

"Wallace has escaped!" the man shouted, jumping up and down. "He's gone to the department store."

"Quick, let's see if we can find him," Mr. Frumbee said, looking worried, and off they ran.

They finally did find Wallace. He was on the main floor in the hat department trying on a smart fedora.

His keeper scolded Wallace for running off, and took him firmly by the hand. But Wallace knew by the way Mr. Frumbee squeezed it that he wasn't really mad.

They smiled at each other and hurried home to the zoo. But Mr. Frumbee didn't lock the cage.

Wallace and Mr. Frumbee enjoyed each other's company. Wallace would ask questions about things that puzzled him, and his keeper would answer as well as he knew how.

"What's the biggest animal in the world?" asked Wallace one day.

"Whales are, then elephants," said his keeper. "But at one time on this earth there were animals far bigger than elephants."

Wallace's bright eyes grew wider.

"They were called dinosaurs, and millions of years ago they walked on this very ground.

"In fact," continued Mr. Frumbee, "you can see their bones in the Nature Museum across the park."

"Oh, really," said Wallace thoughtfully.

"There go the seals barking for their lunch," said Mr. Frumbee, and he hurried off.

Quickly Wallace put on his new suit, slipped through the unlocked cage door, and scurried off to the museum.

It wasn't long before a woman discovered the empty cage and shrieked, "Wallace is gone!"

"And I think I know where," said his keeper, running up.

The chase was on again.

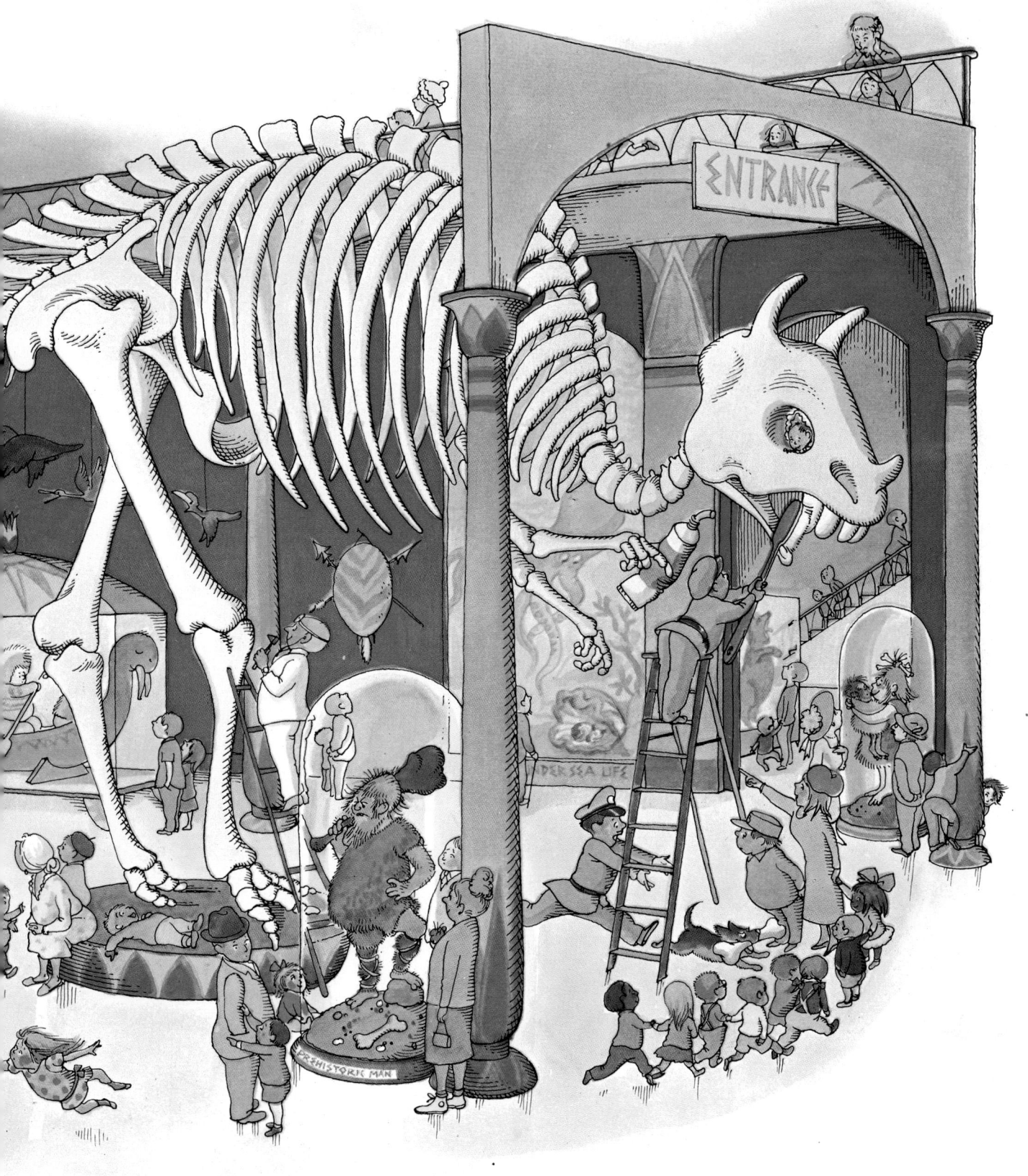

Nearly an hour later they discovered Wallace in the arms of a prehistoric mother made of wax.

Mr. Frumbee smiled to himself, took Wallace by the hand, and led him back to the zoo.

That month the air was warm and gentle. Everyone seemed in a happy, thoughtful mood.

"What a day for a picnic and a drive in the country," said Mr. Frumbee dreamily.

"Picnic? Country?" asked Wallace.

"The streets of the city, over there," explained Mr. Frumbee, "lead you to the country roads where grass and trees and wild flowers grow. You can take your lunch in a basket and eat on the grass."

"How lovely," sighed Wallace, watching the cars go by.

"I must be off and paint the roof of the ostrich house," said the keeper, and he disappeared around a corner.

He waited a few minutes, then looked out in time to see Wallace jump over the zoo wall and into the back seat of a car.

Mr. Frumbee, trying not to smile, cried, "Wallace has escaped again!"

Several alarmed onlookers and the keeper leaped into a cab, all saying at once, "Follow that car."

After some time they found Wallace picnicking with some cows and a little girl.

They drove home after everyone had a taste of picnic lunch, and Wallace was put back in his cage once more.

Early one morning before the zoo had opened, Wallace and Mr. Frumbee were talking while having a breakfast of bananas and tea. Their conversation was interrupted by the bellowing of elephants. It wasn't from the zoo, though, but from a parade passing by.

"A circus parade on its way to the arena," said the keeper. "How I remember loving the circus as a boy."

"What's a circus?" asked Wallace.

"Well, it's a little of everything," answered Mr. Frumbee. "People flying through the air, bears on bicycles, horses dancing."

It sounded too wonderful to be true to Wallace. He couldn't wait for his keeper to start his errands.

Soon he was out of sight, and Wallace was into his clothes and through the unlocked door.

Three small boys saw him running down the street, and they called the keeper.

"Wallace is loose!" they shouted.

"Quick, boys," said Mr. Frumbee, "come with me to the circus and we'll find him."

There was Wallace on the shoulders of a man. He was supporting a whirling constellation on the tip of his finger.

After the act he walked off hand in hand with his keeper to thunderous applause from the audience.

That night Wallace wondered where he would go next.

One day Wallace and Mr. Frumbee were reading the newspaper. Wallace was staring with confusion at the sports page.

"Tell me," he said, dropping his paper and looking up, "what is baseball all about?"

The keeper explained it as well as he knew how. It seemed to satisfy Wallace, for he went back to reading with a knowing smile.

His eye fell on an announcement.

Yawning widely Wallace said, "I think I'll nap for an hour or so."

His keeper, who knew exactly what Wallace was up to, went off about his business.

Before a half hour had passed, Mr. Frumbee heard a familiar cry.

"Wallace has run off!"

A group soon gathered and hurried to the ball park with the keeper in the lead.

It took some time before Wallace was discovered signing autographs near home plate.

Everyone had a hot dog and went happily arm in arm back to the zoo.

One warm day Wallace was fanning himself and listening to his radio when the announcer gave the weather report: "Heat wave hits city. Record crowds are expected at the nearby beaches."

The keeper came by with a lemonade for Wallace.

"What are beaches, Mr. Frumbee?"

"Outside the city some of the land is made of sand instead of earth. It goes down into the sea, and in the summer people go there to play and swim and cool off."

"Oh," said Wallace, sipping his drink and wondering why it didn't refresh him.

"Perhaps I need a dip in the sea," he thought.

Mr. Frumbee took the empty glass, winked at Wallace, and walked away.

In no time at all Wallace was on the back of a bicycle of a family that was obviously going to the beach.

The keeper was soon in hot pursuit, crying, "Wallace is out again!"

9

It was difficult to find Wallace this time, since he was buried up to his neck in the sand.

Mr. Frumbee pulled him out, brushed him off, and after a refreshing swim they returned to their home in the zoo.

COME TO THE

AMUSEMENT PARK!

Rides! Thrills! Games!
Fireworks!

One late afternoon when the crowds had gone and Wallace was alone, he heard a plane overhead and looked up.

His keeper saw it too and knew he would have a busy evening ahead of him.

By the time the sun had set, Wallace was in his suit and on a street corner asking a policeman for directions to the amusement park.

The policeman later realized his terrible mistake and hurried to the zoo to alert Mr. Frumbee.

"Wallace has run away!" he yelled, waving his arms.

Mr. Frumbee quickly boarded a bus and was off on another hunt.

Mr. Frumbee spotted Wallace after a long search. He was in the sideshow as the Wild Man of Borneo. Together they went on some rides, then came back exhausted to their beds in the zoo.

One day the usual crowd of Wallace's friends circled his cage. Mr. Frumbee was washing the floor as Wallace gazed at the fine apartment houses beyond the zoo wall.

"A home with carpets and chairs and curtains," sighed Wallace.

The crowd looked disturbed and whispered among themselves.

"I need some fresh water," said Wallace's keeper, hopping down from the cage.

He knew Wallace would be gone by the time he returned.

There were only two little girls left when he got back to the empty cage.

"Where's Wallace?" they wailed.

"I'll show you," said Mr. Frumbee, and taking their hands, ran to the apartment house.

There they searched and searched . . .

and searched and searched . . .

. . . and searched!

Finally they gave up. They just couldn't find him. Wallace was not there.

The keeper thanked the little girls for helping and went back to stare sadly into Wallace's empty cage.

But the cage wasn't empty. There was Wallace in an overstuffed chair. A carpet was on the floor. There were lamps and curtains and many friends.

A bewildered Mr. Frumbee climbed into the cage.

"Your chair," said Wallace, waving to a rocker. The keeper sat down and said with relief, "We thought you had gone forever, that you would never come back."

"I was off helping my dear friends bring back these fine furnishings they so generously offered me," Wallace said as he put his arm around Mr. Frumbee. "This is my home and favorite place."

His bright black eyes looked through the bars and beyond the tall buildings that surrounded the zoo.

"At least for a while."

Everyone smiled.